Dear Reader,

Did you know there's a Magic Tree House® book for every kid? From those just starting to read chapter books to more experienced readers, Magic Tree House® has something for everyone, including science, sports, geography, wildlife, history... and always a bit of mystery and magic!

Magic Tree House®
Adventures with Jack and Annie, perfect for readers who are just starting to read chapter books.
F&P Levels: M–N

**Magic Tree House®
Merlin Missions**
More challenging adventures for the experienced Magic Tree House® reader.
F&P Levels: M–N

**Magic Tree House®
Super Edition**
A longer and more dangerous adventure with Jack and Annie.
F&P Level: P

**Magic Tree House®
Fact Trackers**
Nonfiction companions to your favorite Magic Tree House® adventures.
F&P Levels: N–T

Happy reading!

Mary Pope Osborne

Magic Tree House®

MAGIC TREE HOUSE®

2 Books in 1!

#1 *Dinosaurs Before Dark*

#2 *The Knight at Dawn*

BY MARY POPE OSBORNE
ILLUSTRATED BY SAL MURDOCCA

A STEPPING STONE BOOK™
Random House 🏠 New York

Text copyright © 1992, 1993, 2012, 2013 by Mary Pope Osborne
Cover art and interior illustrations copyright © 1992, 1993, 2012, 2013 by Sal Murdocca

All rights reserved. Published in the United States by Random House Children's Books, a division of Penguin Random House LLC, New York.

Random House and the colophon are registered trademarks and A Stepping Stone Book and the colophon are trademarks of Penguin Random House LLC. Magic Tree House is a registered trademark of Mary Pope Osborne; used under license.

Visit us on the Web!
rhcbooks.com
MagicTreeHouse.com

Educators and librarians, for a variety of teaching tools,
visit us at RHTeachersLibrarians.com

The Library of Congress has cataloged the individual books under the following Control Numbers: 91-51106 (*Dinosaurs Before Dark*) and 92-13705 (*The Knight at Dawn*).

ISBN 978-0-593-90154-0 (trade)

Printed in the United States of America
10 9 8 7 6 5 4 3 2 1

This book has been officially leveled by using the F&P Text Level Gradient™ Leveling System.

CONTENTS

MARY POPE OSBORNE
MAGIC TREE HOUSE®

#1 DINOSAURS BEFORE DARK

For Linda and Mallory,
who took the trip with me.

CONTENTS

CHAPTER ONE

INTO THE WOODS

"Help! A monster!" said Annie.

"Yeah, sure," said Jack. "A real monster in Frog Creek, Pennsylvania."

"Run, Jack!" said Annie. She ran up the road.

Oh, brother, thought Jack. This is what he got for spending time with his seven-year-old sister.

Annie loved pretend stuff. But Jack was eight and a half. He liked *real* things.

"Watch out, Jack! The monster's coming!" said Annie.

1

Jack didn't say anything.

"Come on, Jack, I'll race you!" said Annie.

"No, thanks," said Jack.

Annie raced alone into the woods.

Jack looked at the sky. The sun was about to set.

"Come on, Annie! It's time to go home!" yelled Jack.

But Annie didn't answer.

Jack waited.

"Annie!" he called again.

"Jack! Jack!" Annie shouted. "Come here! Quick!"

Jack groaned. "This better be good," he said.

Jack left the road and headed into the woods. The trees were lit with a golden late-afternoon light.

"Over here!" called Annie.

2

Annie was standing under a tall oak tree. "Look!" she said. She pointed at a rope ladder. It was hanging down from high in the tree.

"Wow," Jack whispered.

At the top of the tree was a tree house, tucked between two branches.

"That must be the highest tree house in the world," said Annie.

"Who built it?" asked Jack. "I've never seen it before."

"I don't know. But I'm going up," said Annie.

"No! We don't know who it belongs to," said Jack.

"Just for a teeny minute," said Annie. She started up the ladder.

"Annie, come back!" said Jack.

But Annie kept climbing. She climbed all the way up to the tallest branches.

Jack sighed. "Annie, it's almost dark! We have to go home!"

Annie disappeared inside the tree house.

"Annie!" Jack called.

Jack waited a moment. He was about to call again when Annie poked her head out of the tree house window.

"Books!" Annie shouted.

"What?" Jack said.

"It's filled with books!" said Annie.

Oh, man! Jack thought. He loved books.

Jack pushed his glasses into place. He gripped the sides of the rope ladder and started up.

CHAPTER TWO

THE MONSTER

Jack crawled into the tree house.

"Wow," he said. The tree house *was* filled with books. Books were everywhere—very old books with dusty covers and new books with shiny, bright covers.

"Look," said Annie. "You can see far away." She was peering out the tree house window.

Jack looked out the window with her. Below were the tops of the other trees. In the distance he could see the Frog Creek library and the elementary school and the park.

Annie pointed in the other direction.

"There's our house," she said.

Annie was right. Jack could see their white wooden house with its green porch. In the yard next door was their neighbor's black dog, Henry. He looked very tiny.

"Hi, Henry!" shouted Annie.

"Shush! We're not supposed to be up here," said Jack.

Jack glanced around the tree house again. He noticed that bookmarks were sticking out of many of the books. "I wonder who owns all these books," he said.

"I like this one," said Annie. She picked up a book with a castle on the cover.

"Here's a book about Pennsylvania," said Jack. He turned to the page with the bookmark.

"Hey, here's a picture of Frog Creek," said

Jack. "It's a picture of *these* woods!"

"Oh, here's a book for you," said Annie. She held up a book about dinosaurs. A blue silk bookmark was sticking out of it.

"Let me see," said Jack. He set his backpack down on the floor and grabbed the book from Annie.

"Okay. You look at that one, and I'll look at the one about castles," said Annie.

"No, we'd better not," said Jack. "We don't know who these books belong to."

But even as he said this, Jack was opening the dinosaur book to the place where the bookmark was. He couldn't help himself.

Jack turned to a picture of an ancient flying reptile. He recognized it as a Pteranodon. He touched the huge bat-like wings in the picture.

"Wow," whispered Jack. "I wish we could

go to the time of Pteranodons."

Jack studied the picture of the odd-looking creature soaring through the sky.

"Ahhh!" screamed Annie.

"What?" said Jack.

"A monster!" Annie cried. She pointed out the tree house window.

"Stop pretending, Annie," said Jack.

"No, really!" said Annie.

Jack looked out the window.

A giant creature was gliding above the treetops! It had a long, weird crest on the back of its head, a skinny beak, and huge bat-like wings!

It was a real live Pteranodon!

The creature swooped through the sky. It looked like a glider plane! It was coming straight toward the tree house!

"Get down!" cried Annie.

Jack and Annie crouched on the floor.

The wind started to blow.

The tree house started to spin.

It spun faster and faster.

Then everything was still.

Absolutely still.

CHAPTER THREE

WHERE IS HERE?

Jack opened his eyes. Sunlight slanted through the window.

The tree house was still high up in a tree.

But it wasn't the *same* tree.

"Where are we?" said Annie. She and Jack looked out the window.

The Pteranodon was soaring through the sky. The ground was covered with ferns and tall grass. There was a winding stream, a sloping hill, and volcanoes in the distance.

"I—I don't know where we are," said Jack.

The Pteranodon glided down to the base of the tree. It landed on the ground and stood very still.

"So what just happened to us?" said Annie.

"Well . . . ," said Jack. "I was looking at the picture in the book—"

"And you said, 'Wow, I wish we could go to the time of Pteranodons,' " said Annie.

"Yeah. And then we saw a Pteranodon in the Frog Creek woods," said Jack.

"Yeah. And then the wind got loud. And the tree house started spinning," said Annie.

"And we landed here," said Jack.

"And we landed here," said Annie.

"So that means . . . ," said Jack.

"So that means . . . what?" said Annie.

"I don't know," said Jack. He shook his head. "None of this can be real."

Annie looked out the window again. "But *he*'s real," she said. "He's *very* real."

Jack looked out the window with her again. The Pteranodon was standing at the base of the tree like a guard. His giant wings were spread out on either side of him.

"Hi!" Annie shouted.

"Shhh!" said Jack. "We're not supposed to be here."

"But where is *here*?" said Annie.

"I don't know," said Jack.

"Hi! Who are you?" Annie called to the Pteranodon.

The creature just looked up at her.

"Are you nuts? He can't talk," said Jack. "But maybe the book can tell us."

Jack looked down at the book. He read the words under the picture:

> **This flying reptile lived in the Cretaceous Period. It vanished 65 million years ago with the dinosaurs.**

"That's impossible!" said Jack. "We can't have gone to a time sixty-five million years ago!"

"Jack," said Annie. "He's nice."

"Nice?" said Jack.

"Yeah, I can tell," said Annie. "Let's go down to him."

"Go down?" said Jack.

Annie started down the rope ladder.

"Hey, come back," said Jack.

But Annie kept going.

"Annie, wait!" Jack called.

Annie dropped to the ground. She stepped boldly up to the ancient creature.

CHAPTER FOUR

HENRY

Jack gasped as Annie reached out her hand toward the Pteranodon.

Oh, no, he thought. Annie was always trying to make friends with animals, but this was going too far.

"Don't get too close to him, Annie!" Jack shouted.

Annie touched the Pteranodon's crest. She stroked his neck. She was talking to him.

What in the world is she saying? Jack wondered.

He took a deep breath. Okay. He would go down, too. It would be good to examine a Pteranodon. He could take notes like a scientist.

Jack started down the rope ladder. When he reached the ground, he was only a few feet away from the creature.

The Pteranodon stared at Jack. His eyes were bright and alert.

"He's soft, Jack," said Annie. "He feels like Henry."

Jack snorted. "He's no dog, Annie."

"Feel him, Jack," said Annie.

Jack didn't move.

"Don't think, Jack. Just do it," Annie said.

Jack stepped forward. He reached out very cautiously. He brushed his hand down the creature's neck.

Interesting, Jack thought. A thin layer of

fuzz covered the Pteranodon's skin.

"Soft, huh?" said Annie.

Jack reached into his backpack and pulled out a pencil and a notebook. He wrote:

fuzzy skin

"What are you doing?" asked Annie.

"Taking notes," said Jack. "We're probably the first people in the whole world to ever see a real live Pteranodon."

Jack looked at the Pteranodon again. The bony crest on top of his head was longer than Jack's arm.

"I wonder how smart he is," Jack said.

"*Very* smart," said Annie.

"Don't count on it," said Jack. "His brain's probably no bigger than a bean."

"No, he's very smart. I can feel it," said Annie. "I'm going to call him Henry."

Jack wrote in his notebook:

small brain?

Jack looked at the creature again. "Maybe he's a mutant," he said.

The Pteranodon tilted his head.

Annie laughed. "He's not a mutant, Jack."

"Well, what's he doing here then? Where is this place?" said Jack.

Annie leaned close to the Pteranodon. "Do you know where we are, Henry?" she asked softly.

The creature fixed his eyes on Annie. His long jaws were opening and closing like a giant pair of scissors.

"Are you trying to talk to me, Henry?" asked Annie.

"Forget it, Annie." Jack wrote in his notebook:

mouth like scissors

"Did we come to a time long ago, Henry?"

asked Annie. "Is this a place from long ago?"

Suddenly Annie gasped. "Jack!"

Jack looked up.

Annie was pointing toward the hill. On top stood a huge dinosaur!

CHAPTER FIVE

GOLD IN THE GRASS

"Go! *Go!*" said Jack. He threw his notebook into his pack. He pushed Annie toward the rope ladder.

"Bye, Henry!" she said.

"Go!" said Jack. He gave Annie another push.

"Quit it!" she said. But she started up the ladder. Jack scrambled after her.

Jack and Annie tumbled into the tree house. They were panting as they looked out the window at the dinosaur. It was standing on the hilltop, eating flowers off a tree.

"Oh, man," whispered Jack. "We *are* in a time long ago!"

The dinosaur looked like a huge rhinoceros with three horns instead of one. It had two long horns above its eyes, and another one grew out from its nose. It had a big shield-like thing behind its head.

"Triceratops!" said Jack.

"Does he eat people?" whispered Annie.

"I'll look it up." Jack grabbed the dinosaur book. He flipped through the pages.

"There!" said Jack, pointing to a picture of a Triceratops. He read the caption:

> The Triceratops lived in the late Cretaceous Period. This plant-eating dinosaur weighed over 12,000 pounds.

Jack slammed the book shut. "Just plants. No meat."

"Good!" said Annie. "Let's go see him up close."

"Are you crazy?" said Jack.

"Don't you want to take notes about him?" asked Annie. "We're probably the first people in the whole world to ever see a real live Triceratops."

Jack sighed. Annie was right.

"Okay, let's go," he said.

Jack shoved the dinosaur book into his pack. He slung his pack over his shoulder. Annie started down the ladder, and Jack followed her.

"Just promise you won't pet him," Jack called down to Annie.

"I promise," said Annie.

"Promise you won't kiss him," said Jack.

"I promise," said Annie.

"Promise you won't talk to him."

"I promise," said Annie.

"Promise you won't—"

"Don't worry!" said Annie.

Annie and Jack stepped off the ladder. The Pteranodon gave them a friendly look.

Annie blew him a kiss. "Be back soon, Henry!" she called.

"Shhh!" said Jack. And he led the way slowly and carefully through the ferns.

When Jack and Annie reached the bottom of the hill, they knelt behind a bush. Annie started to speak, but Jack quickly put his finger to his lips. Then he and Annie peeked out at the Triceratops.

The dinosaur was bigger than a truck. He was eating the flowers off a magnolia tree.

Jack slipped his notebook out of his pack. He wrote:

eats flowers

Annie nudged him.

Jack ignored her. He studied the Triceratops again. He wrote:

eats slowly

Annie nudged him harder.

Jack looked at her.

Annie pointed to herself. She walked her fingers through the air. She pointed to the dinosaur. She smiled.

Is she teasing? Jack wondered.

Annie waved at Jack.

Jack started to grab her.

She laughed and jumped away. She fell into the grass in full view of the Triceratops!

"Get back!" whispered Jack.

Too late. The big dinosaur had spotted Annie. He gazed down at her from the hilltop. Half of a magnolia flower was sticking out of his mouth.

"Oops," said Annie.

"Get back!" Jack said again.

"He looks nice, Jack," Annie said.

"Nice? Watch out for his horns, Annie!" said Jack.

The Triceratops gazed calmly down at Annie. Then he turned and loped down the side of the hill.

"Bye!" said Annie. She turned back to Jack. "See?"

Jack grunted. But he wrote in his notebook:

nice

"Come on. Let's look around some more," said Annie.

As Jack started after Annie, he saw something glittering in the tall grass.

Jack reached down and picked it up. It was
a gold medallion.

A letter was engraved on the medallion: a fancy *M*.

"Oh, man. Someone was here before us!" Jack said softly.

CHAPTER SIX

DINOSAUR VALLEY

"Annie, look at this!" Jack called. "Look what I found!"

Annie had gone up to the hilltop. She was picking a flower from the magnolia tree.

"Annie, look! A medallion!" shouted Jack.

But Annie wasn't paying attention to Jack. She was staring at something on the other side of the hill.

"Oh, wow!" she said. Clutching her magnolia flower, she took off down the hill.

"Annie, come back!" Jack shouted.

But Annie had disappeared.

"Oh, brother," Jack muttered. He stuffed the gold medallion into his jeans pocket.

Then Jack heard Annie shriek.

"Annie?" he said.

Jack heard another sound as well—a deep, bellowing sound, like a tuba.

"Jack! Come here, quick!" Annie called.

Jack raced up the hill. When he got to the top, he gasped.

The valley below was filled with nests— big nests made out of mud. The nests were filled with tiny dinosaurs!

Annie was crouching next to one of the nests. Towering over her was a gigantic duck-billed dinosaur!

"Don't panic. Don't move," said Jack. He stepped slowly down the hill toward Annie.

The huge dinosaur was waving her arms and making her tuba sound.

Jack stopped. He didn't want to get too close.

He knelt on the ground. "Okay. Move toward me. Slowly," he said.

Annie started to stand up.

"Don't stand! Crawl," said Jack.

Clutching her flower, Annie crawled toward Jack.

Still bellowing, the duck-billed dinosaur followed her.

Annie froze.

"Keep going," Jack said.

Annie started crawling again.

Jack inched farther down the hill, until he was just an arm's distance from Annie. He reached out and grabbed her hand. He pulled Annie toward him.

"Stay down," Jack said. He crouched next to her. "Bow your head. Pretend to chew."

"Chew?" said Annie.

"Yes," said Jack. "I read that's what you

do if a mean dog comes at you."

"She's no dog, Jack," said Annie.

"Just chew," said Jack.

Jack and Annie both bowed their heads and pretended to chew. Soon the dinosaur grew quiet.

Jack looked up. "I don't think she's mad anymore," he said.

"You saved me," said Annie. "Thanks."

"You have to use your brain, Annie," said Jack. "You can't just go running to a nest of babies. There's always a mother nearby."

Annie stood up.

"Annie, don't!" said Jack.

Too late.

Annie held out her magnolia flower to the dinosaur.

"I'm sorry I made you worry about your babies," she said.

The dinosaur moved closer to Annie.

She grabbed the flower from her hand. She reached for another.

"No more," said Annie.

The dinosaur let out a sad tuba sound.

"But there are more flowers up there," Annie said. She pointed to the top of the hill. "I'll get you some."

Annie hurried up the hill.

The dinosaur waddled after her.

Jack quickly looked at the dinosaur babies. Some were crawling out of their nests.

Where are the other mothers? Jack wondered.

Jack took out the dinosaur book. He flipped through the pages. He found a picture of some duck-billed dinosaurs. He read the caption:

The Anatosauruses lived in colonies. While a few mothers babysat the nests, others looked for food.

So there were probably more mothers close by, looking for food.

"Hey, Jack!" Annie called.

Jack looked up. Annie was at the top of the hill, feeding magnolia flowers to the giant Anatosaurus!

"Guess what?" Annie said. "She's nice, too."

Suddenly the Anatosaurus made her terrible tuba sound. Annie crouched down and started to chew.

The dinosaur charged down the hill. She seemed afraid of something.

Jack put the book on top of his pack. He hurried to Annie.

"I wonder why she ran away," said Annie. "We were starting to be friends."

Jack looked around. What he saw in the distance almost made him faint!

An enormous monster was coming across the plain.

The monster was walking on two strong legs. It was swinging a long, thick tail and dangling two tiny arms.

It had a huge head—and its jaws were wide open.

Even from far away Jack could see its long, gleaming teeth.

"Tyrannosaurus rex!" whispered Jack.

CHAPTER SEVEN

READY, SET, GO!

"Run, Annie! Run!" cried Jack. "Run to the tree house!"

Jack and Annie dashed down the hill together. They ran through the tall grass and ferns and past the Pteranodon.

They scrambled up the rope ladder and tumbled into the tree house.

Annie leaped to the window.

"It's going away!" she said, panting.

Jack pushed his glasses into place. He looked out the window with Annie.

The Tyrannosaurus was wandering off.

But then the monster stopped and turned around.

"Duck!" said Jack.

The two of them ducked their heads.

After a long moment, they peeked out the window again.

"Coast clear," said Jack.

"Yay," whispered Annie.

"We have to get out of here," said Jack.

"You made a wish before," said Annie.

"Right," said Jack. He took a deep breath. "I wish we could go back to Frog Creek!"

Nothing happened.

"I said I wish—" started Jack.

"Wait," said Annie. "You were looking at a picture in the dinosaur book. Remember?"

"Oh, no, I left the book and my pack on the hill!" said Jack. "I have to go back!"

"Forget it," said Annie.

"I can't," said Jack. "The book doesn't belong to us. Plus my notebook with all my notes is in my pack. And my—"

"Okay, okay!" said Annie.

"I'll hurry!" said Jack. He climbed quickly down the ladder and leaped to the ground.

Jack raced past the Pteranodon, through the ferns, through the tall grass, and up the hill.

He looked down.

His pack was lying on the ground. On top of it was the dinosaur book.

But now the valley below was filled with Anatosauruses. They were all standing guard around the nests.

Where had they been? Did fear of the Tyrannosaurus send them home?

Jack took a deep breath. *Ready! Set! Go!* he thought.

He charged down the hill. He ran to his backpack. He scooped it up. He grabbed the dinosaur book.

Jack heard a terrible tuba sound! Then another, and another! All the Anatosauruses were bellowing at him!

Jack took off.

He raced up to the hilltop.

He started down the hill.

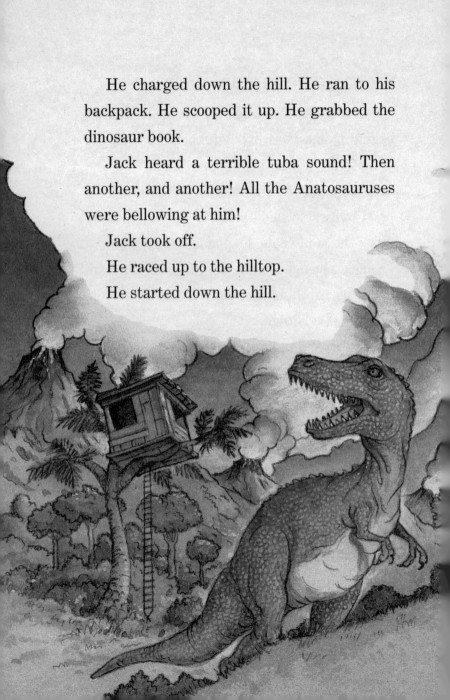

He stopped.

The Tyrannosaurus rex was back! It was standing between Jack and the tree house!

CHAPTER EIGHT

A GIANT SHADOW

Jack jumped behind the magnolia tree.

His heart was beating so fast he could hardly think.

He peeked out at the giant monster. The horrible-looking creature was opening and closing its huge jaws. Its teeth were as big as steak knives.

Don't panic, thought Jack. *Think*.

He peered down at the valley.

Good. The duck-billed dinosaurs were sticking close to their nests.

Jack looked back at the Tyrannosaurus.

Good. The monster still didn't seem to know he was there.

Don't panic. Think. Think. Maybe there's information in the book.

Jack opened the dinosaur book. He found Tyrannosaurus rex. He read:

> **Tyrannosaurus rex was one of the largest meat-eating land animals of all time. If it were alive today, it could eat a human in one bite.**

Great, thought Jack. The book was no help at all.

Jack tried to think clearly. He couldn't hide on the other side of the hill. The Anatosauruses might stampede.

He couldn't run to the tree house. The

47

Tyrannosaurus might run faster.

Maybe he should just wait for the monster to leave.

Jack peeked around the tree.

The Tyrannosaurus had wandered *closer* to the hill.

Something caught Jack's eye. Annie was coming down the rope ladder!

Is she nuts? What is she doing? Jack wondered.

Jack watched Annie hop off the ladder.

Annie hurried over to the Pteranodon. She was talking to him. She was flapping her arms. She pointed at Jack, at the sky, at the tree house.

She is *nuts!* Jack thought.

"Go! Go back up in the tree!" Jack whispered. "Go!"

Jack heard a roar.

The Tyrannosaurus rex was looking in his direction.

Jack hit the ground.

The Tyrannosaurus rex was coming toward the hill.

Jack felt the ground shaking.

What should I do? Jack wondered. *Should I run? Crawl back into Dinosaur Valley? Climb the magnolia tree?*

Suddenly a giant shadow covered Jack. He looked up.

The Pteranodon was gliding overhead. The giant creature sailed toward the top of the hill.

He was heading toward Jack.

CHAPTER NINE

THE AMAZING RIDE

The Pteranodon coasted down to the ground.

He stared at Jack with his bright, alert eyes.

What was Jack supposed to do? Climb on? *But I'm too heavy,* thought Jack.

Jack looked at the Tyrannosaurus. It was starting up the hill. Its giant teeth were flashing in the sunlight.

Okay, thought Jack. *Don't think! Just do it!*

Jack put his book in his pack. Then he climbed onto the Pteranodon's back. He held on tightly.

The creature moved forward. He spread his wings—and lifted off the ground!

Jack nearly fell off as they teetered this way and that.

The Pteranodon steadied himself and rose into the sky.

Jack looked down. The Tyrannosaurus was staring up at him and chomping the air.

The Pteranodon glided away.

He sailed over the hilltop and over the valley.

He circled above all the duck-billed dinosaurs and all the nests filled with babies.

Then the Pteranodon soared out over the plain—over the Triceratops, who was grazing in the high grass.

Jack felt like a bird. The wind was rushing through his hair. The air smelled sweet and fresh.

Jack whooped and laughed. He couldn't believe it! He was riding on the back of an ancient flying reptile!

The Pteranodon sailed over the stream and over the ferns and bushes. Then he carried Jack down to the base of the oak tree.

When they came to a stop, Jack slid off the creature's back and landed on the ground.

The Pteranodon took off again and glided into the sky.

"Bye, Henry!" called Jack.

"Jack! Are you okay?" Annie shouted from the tree house.

Jack pushed his glasses into place. He kept staring at the Pteranodon.

"Jack!" Annie called.

Jack looked up at Annie. He smiled.

"Thanks for saving my life," he said. "That was really fun."

"Thank Henry, not me!" said Annie. "Come on! Climb up!"

Jack tried to stand. His legs were wobbly. He felt a bit dizzy.

"Hurry!" shouted Annie. "It's coming!"

Jack looked around. The Tyrannosaurus

was heading straight toward him! Jack bolted to the ladder. He started climbing.

"Hurry! Hurry!" screamed Annie.

Jack reached the top and scrambled into the tree house.

"It's coming toward the tree!" Annie cried.

The dinosaur slammed against the oak tree. The tree house shook like a leaf in the wind.

Jack and Annie tumbled into the books.

"Make a wish to go home!" cried Annie.

"We need the book! The Pennsylvania book!" said Jack. "Where is it?"

They both searched madly around the tree house.

"Found it!" said Jack.

He grabbed the book and flipped through the pages. He found the photograph of the Frog Creek woods.

Jack pointed to the picture in the book.

"I wish we could go home!" he shouted.

The wind began to blow.

Jack closed his eyes. He held on tightly to Annie.

The tree house started to spin.

It spun faster and faster.

Then everything was still.

Absolutely still.

CHAPTER TEN

HOME BEFORE DARK

Jack heard a bird singing.

He opened his eyes. He was still pointing at the picture of the Frog Creek woods.

He peeked out the tree house window. Outside he saw the exact same view as the picture in the book.

"We're home," whispered Annie.

The woods were lit with a golden late-afternoon light. The sun was about to set.

No time had passed since they'd left Frog Creek.

"Ja-ack! An-nie!" a voice called from the distance.

"That's Mom," said Annie.

Jack saw their mother far away. She was standing in front of their house. She looked tiny.

"An-nie! Ja-ack!" she called.

Annie stuck her head out the window and shouted, "Coming!"

Jack still felt dazed. He just stared at Annie.

"What happened to us?" he said.

"We took a trip in a magic tree house," said Annie simply.

"But it's the same time as when we left," said Jack.

Annie shrugged.

"How did it take us so far away?" said Jack. "And so long ago?"

"You looked at a picture in a book and said you wished we could go there," said Annie. "And the magic tree house took us there."

"But *how*?" said Jack. "And who built this magic tree house? Who put all these books here?"

"A magic person, I guess," said Annie.

"Oh, look," said Jack. "I almost forgot about this."

Jack reached into his pocket and pulled out the gold medallion. "Someone lost this back there," he said, "in dinosaur land. Look, there's a letter *M* on it."

Annie's eyes got round. "You think *M* stands for *magic person*?" she asked.

"I don't know," said Jack. "I just know someone went to that place before us."

"Ja-ack! An-nie!" their mom called again.

"Coming!" Annie shouted again.

Jack put the gold medallion back in his pocket. He pulled the dinosaur book out of his pack and put it back with all the other books.

Then he and Annie took one last look around the tree house.

"Good-bye, house," whispered Annie.

Jack slung his backpack over his shoulders.

Annie started down the rope ladder. Jack followed.

Seconds later they hopped onto the ground and started walking out of the woods.

"No one's going to believe our story," said Jack.

"So let's not tell anyone," said Annie.

"Dad won't believe it," said Jack.

"He'll say it was a dream," said Annie.

"Mom won't believe it," said Jack.

"She'll say it was pretend."

"My teacher won't believe it," said Jack.

"She'll say you're nuts," said Annie.

"We'd better not tell anyone," said Jack.

"I already said that," said Annie.

Jack sighed. "I think I'm starting not to believe it myself," he said.

They left the woods and started up the road toward their house.

As they walked past all the houses on their street, the trip to dinosaur time *did* seem more and more like a dream.

Only *this* world and *this* time seemed real.

Jack reached into his pocket. He clasped the gold medallion.

He felt the engraving of the letter *M*. It made his fingers tingle.

Jack laughed. Suddenly he felt very happy.

He couldn't explain what had happened today. But he knew for sure that their trip in the magic tree house had been real.

Absolutely real.

"Tomorrow," Jack said softly, "we'll go back to the woods."

"Of course," said Annie.

"And we'll climb up to the tree house," said Jack.

"Of course," said Annie.

"And we'll see what happens next," said Jack.

"Of course," said Annie. "Race you!"

And they took off together, running for home.

For Nathaniel Pope

CONTENTS

CHAPTER ONE

THE DARK WOODS

Jack couldn't sleep.

He put his glasses on. He looked at the clock. It was five-thirty.

Too early to get up.

Yesterday so many strange things had happened. Now he was trying to figure them out.

He turned on the light. He picked up his notebook. He looked at the list he'd made before going to bed.

found tree house in woods

found lots of books in it

pointed to Pteranodon
picture in book

made a wish

went to time of dinosaurs

pointed to a picture of
Frog Creek woods

made a wish

came home to Frog Creek

Jack pushed his glasses into place. Who was going to believe any of this?

His mom wouldn't believe it. Neither would his dad or his third-grade teacher, Ms. Watkins. Only his seven-year-old sister, Annie, understood. She'd gone with him to the time of the dinosaurs.

"Can't you sleep?"

Annie was standing in his doorway.

"Nope," said Jack.

"Me neither," said Annie. "What are you doing?"

She walked over to Jack and looked at his notebook. She read the list.

"Aren't you going to write about the gold medal?" she asked.

"You mean the gold medallion," said Jack.

He picked up his pencil and wrote:

found this in dinosaur time

"Aren't you going to put the letter M on the medal?" said Annie.

"Medallion," said Jack. "Not medal."

He added an M:

"Aren't you going to write about the magic person?" said Annie.

"We don't know for sure if there is a magic person," said Jack.

"Well, someone built the tree house in the woods, and someone put the books in it. Someone lost a gold medal in dinosaur time," said Annie.

"Medallion!" said Jack for the third time. "And I'm just writing the facts. The stuff we know for sure."

"Let's go back to the tree house right now," said Annie, "and find out if the magic person is a fact."

"Are you nuts?" said Jack. "The sun's not even up yet."

"Come on," said Annie. "Maybe we can catch them sleeping."

"I don't think we should go there," said Jack. He was worried. What if the "magic person" was mean? What if he or she didn't want kids to know about the tree house?

"Well, I'm going," said Annie.

Jack looked out his window at the dark gray sky. It was almost dawn.

He sighed. "Okay. Go get dressed. I'll meet you at the back door. Be quiet."

"Yay!" whispered Annie. She tiptoed away as quietly as a mouse.

Jack put on jeans, a warm sweatshirt, and sneakers. He tossed his notebook and pencil in his backpack.

He crept downstairs.

Annie was waiting by the back door. She shined a flashlight in Jack's face. "Ta-da! A magic wand!" she said.

"Shhh! Don't wake up Mom and Dad," whispered Jack. "And turn that flashlight off. We don't want anyone to see us."

Annie nodded and turned the flashlight off. Then she clipped it onto her belt.

Jack and Annie slipped out the door into the cool early-morning air. Crickets were chirping. The dog next door barked.

"Quiet, Henry!" whispered Annie.

Henry stopped barking. Animals always seemed to do what Annie said.

"Let's run!" said Jack.

Jack and Annie dashed across the dark, wet lawn and didn't stop until they reached the Frog Creek woods.

"We need the flashlight now," said Jack.

Annie took it off her belt and switched it on.

Step by step, she and Jack walked between the trees. Jack held his breath. The dark woods were a little scary.

"Gotcha!" said Annie, shining the flashlight in Jack's face.

Jack jumped back. Then he frowned.

"Cut it out!" he said.

"I scared you," said Annie.

Jack glared at her.

"Stop pretending!" he whispered. "This is serious."

"Okay, okay."

Annie shined her flashlight into the tops of the trees.

"Now what are you doing?" said Jack.

"Looking for the tree house!"

The light stopped moving.

The mysterious tree house sat high in the branches of the tallest tree in the woods.

Annie shined her light down the long rope ladder.

"I'm going up," she said. Still holding the flashlight, she began to climb.

"Wait!" Jack called.

What if someone was in the tree house?

"Annie! Come back!"

But Annie was gone. The light had disappeared.

Jack was alone in the dark.

CHAPTER TWO

LEAVING AGAIN

"Annie!" Jack shouted.

"No one's here!" she shouted back.

Jack thought about going home. Then he thought about all the books in the tree house.

He started up the ladder. When he was almost at the top, he saw light in the distant sky. Dawn was starting to break.

Jack crawled through a hole in the tree house floor and took off his backpack.

Annie shined her flashlight on the books scattered about the floor.

"They're still here," she said.

Annie shined the light on a dinosaur book. It was the book that had taken them to the time of dinosaurs.

"Remember the Tyrannosaurus rex?" asked Annie.

Jack shuddered. Of course he remembered! How could anyone forget seeing a real live Tyrannosaurus rex?

The light fell on a book about Pennsylvania. A red silk bookmark stuck out of it.

"Remember the picture of Frog Creek?" said Annie.

"Of course," said Jack. That was the picture that had brought them home.

"There's my favorite," said Annie.

The light was shining on a book about knights and castles. There was a blue leather bookmark in it.

Annie turned to the page with the bookmark.

There was a picture of a knight on a black horse. He was riding toward a castle.

"Annie, close that book," said Jack. "I know what you're thinking."

Annie pointed at the cover.

"Don't, Annie!" said Jack.

"We wish we could go there," Annie said.

"No, we don't!" shouted Jack.

The wind began to moan. The leaves began to tremble.

It was happening again.

"We're leaving!" cried Annie. "Get down!"

The wind moaned louder. The leaves shook harder.

Jack squeezed his eyes shut.

The tree house started to spin.

It spun faster and faster!

Then everything was still.

Absolutely still.

❧ ❧ ❧

Jack opened his eyes. He shivered. The air was damp and cool.

The sound of a horse's whinny came from below.

Neeee-hhhh!

"I think we're here," whispered Annie. She was still holding the castle book.

Jack peeked out the window.

A huge castle loomed out of the fog.

Jack looked around. The tree house was in a different oak tree.

"Look!" said Annie.

Down below, a knight on a black horse was riding by.

"Oh, man," said Jack, "that's incredible. But—we can't stay here. We have to go home and make a plan first." He picked up the book about Pennsylvania. He opened it to the page with the red silk bookmark. He pointed to the photograph of the Frog Creek woods. "I wish—"

"No!" said Annie. She yanked the book away from him. "Let's stay! I want to visit the castle!"

"You're nuts. We need to examine the situation," said Jack. "From home."

"Let's examine it here!" said Annie.

"Come on, Annie." Jack held out his hand. "Give it."

Annie gave Jack the book. "Okay. You can go home. I'm staying," she said. She clipped the flashlight to her belt.

"Wait!" said Jack.

"I'm going to take a peek. A teeny peek," she said. And she scooted down the ladder.

Jack groaned. *Okay, Annie won.* He couldn't leave without her. Besides, he sort of wanted to take a peek himself.

Jack put down the book about Pennsylvania. He dropped the castle book into his pack. He stepped onto the ladder and headed into the cool, misty air.

CHAPTER THREE

ACROSS THE BRIDGE

Annie was under the tree, looking across the foggy ground.

"The knight's riding toward that bridge, I think," said Annie. "The bridge goes to the castle."

"Wait. I'll look it up," said Jack. "Give me the flashlight!"

He took the flashlight from Annie and pulled the castle book out of his pack. He opened it to the page with the leather bookmark.

He read the words under the picture of the knight:

> **This is a knight arriving for a castle feast. Knights wore armor when they traveled long and dangerous distances. Armor was very heavy. A tournament helmet could weigh up to forty pounds.**

Wow. Jack had weighed forty pounds when he was five. *It would be like riding a horse with a five-year-old on your head!* he thought.

Jack pulled out his notebook. He wanted to take notes, as he'd done on their dinosaur trip.

He wrote:

heavy head

What else?

He turned the pages of the castle book. He found a picture that showed the whole castle and the buildings around it.

"The knight's crossing the bridge," said Annie. "He's going through the gate. . . . He's gone."

Jack studied the bridge in the picture.

He read:

A drawbridge crossed the moat.
The moat was filled with water, to
help protect the castle from enemies.
Some people believe crocodiles were
kept in the moat.

Jack wrote in his notebook:

crocodiles in moat?

"Look!" said Annie, peering through the

mist. "A windmill! Right over there!"

"Yeah, there's a windmill in here, too," said Jack, pointing at the picture.

"Look at the *real* one, Jack," said Annie. "Not the one in the book."

A piercing shriek split the air.

"Yikes," said Annie. "It sounded like it came from that little house over there!" She pointed through the fog.

"There's a little house *here*," said Jack, studying the picture. He turned the page and read:

> **The hawk house was in the inner ward of the castle. Hawks were trained to hunt other birds and small animals.**

Jack wrote in his notebook:

hawks in hawk house

"We must be in the inner ward," said Jack.

"Listen!" whispered Annie. "Do you hear that? Drums! Horns! They're coming from the castle. Let's go see!"

"Wait," said Jack. He turned more pages of the book.

"I want to see what's *really* going on, Jack. Not what's in the book," said Annie.

"But look at this!" said Jack.

He pointed to a picture of a big party. Men were standing by the door, playing drums and horns.

He read:

Feasts were held in the Great Hall. Fanfares were played to announce different dishes in a feast.

"You can look at the book. I'm going to the real feast," said Annie.

"Wait," said Jack, studying the picture. It showed boys his age carrying trays of food. On the trays were peacocks with all their feathers, whole pigs, and pies.

Peacocks? Jack thought.

He wrote:

they eat peacocks?

Jack held up the book to show Annie. "Look, I think they eat—"

Where was she?

Jack looked through the fog.

He heard the real drums and the real horns. He saw the real hawk house, the real windmill, the real moat.

He saw Annie dashing across the real drawbridge. Then she vanished through the gate leading to the castle.

CHAPTER FOUR

INTO THE CASTLE

"Oh, brother," muttered Jack.

He threw his stuff into his pack and moved toward the drawbridge. He hoped no one would see him.

It was getting darker.

When Jack got to the bridge, he started across. The wooden planks creaked under his feet. He peered over the edge of the bridge. *Are there any crocodiles in the moat?* he wondered. He couldn't tell.

"Halt!" someone shouted. A guard on top of the castle wall was looking down.

Jack dashed across the bridge. He ran through the castle gate and into the courtyard. He heard the sounds of music, shouting, and laughter.

Jack hurried to a dark corner and crouched down. He shivered as he looked for Annie.

Torches lit the high wall around the courtyard. The courtyard was nearly empty.

Two boys led horses that clopped over the gray cobblestones. One of them was the knight's black horse.

"Psssst! Jack!"

Jack peered into the darkness.

There was Annie.

She was hiding behind a well in the center of the courtyard. She waved at him.

Jack waved back. He waited until the boys

and horses disappeared inside the stable. Then
he dashed to the well.

"I'm going to find the music!" whispered
Annie. "Are you coming?"

"Okay," Jack said with a sigh.

They tiptoed together across the cobblestones. Then they slipped through the entrance
of the castle.

Laughter and music came from a bright
room in front of them. They stood at the doorway and peeked in.

"The feast in the Great Hall!" whispered Jack. He held his breath as he stared in awe.

A giant fireplace blazed at one end of the noisy room. Antlers and rugs hung on the stone walls. Flowers covered the floor.

People in bright clothes and funny hats strolled among the crowd. Some played oddly shaped guitars. Some juggled balls in the air. Some balanced swords on their hands.

Boys in short dresses carried huge trays of food. Dogs were fighting over bones under the tables. Men and women dressed in capes and furs sat at long, crowded wooden tables.

"I wonder which one is the knight," said Jack.

"I don't know," whispered Annie. "But look—they're all eating with their fingers!"

"Halt!" someone shouted behind them.

Jack whirled around.

A man carrying a tray of pies was standing a few feet away.

"Who art thou?" he asked angrily.

"Jack," squeaked Jack.

"Annie," squeaked Annie.

Then they ran as fast as they could down a dimly lit hallway.

CHAPTER FIVE

TRAPPED

"Come on!" cried Annie. "Hurry!"

Jack raced behind her.

"Here! Quick!" Annie dashed toward a door off the hallway. She pushed the door open. Jack and Annie stumbled into a dark, cold room. The door creaked shut behind them.

"Give me the flashlight," said Annie. Jack handed it to her, and she switched it on.

"Yikes!" said Annie. A row of knights was right in front of them!

Annie flicked off the light.

Silence.

"They aren't moving," Jack whispered.

Annie switched the light back on.

"They're just suits," Jack said.

"Without heads," said Annie.

"Let me have the flashlight for a second," said Jack. "So I can look in the book."

Annie handed Jack the flashlight. He pulled out the castle book. He flipped through the pages until he found what he was looking for.

Jack put the book away. "It's called the armory," he said. "It's where armor and weapons are stored."

He shined the flashlight around the room.

"Oh, man," whispered Jack.

The light fell on shiny breastplates, leg plates, and arm plates. Shelves were filled with helmets and weapons. Shields, spears, swords, crossbows, clubs, and battle-axes hung on the walls.

Voices came from the hallway.

"Let's hide!" said Annie.

"Wait," said Jack. "I've got to check on something first."

"Hurry," said Annie.

"It'll take just a second," said Jack. "Hold this." He handed Annie the flashlight.

He tried to lift a helmet from a shelf. It was too heavy.

He bent down and dragged the helmet over his head. The visor slammed shut.

Oh, man, thought Jack. *This is worse than having a five-year-old on my head. It's like having a* ten-*year-old on my head!*

Not only could Jack not lift his head, he couldn't see anything, either.

"Jack!" Annie sounded far away. "They're getting closer!"

"Turn off the flashlight!" Jack's voice echoed inside the metal helmet.

He struggled to get the helmet off.

Suddenly he lost his balance and went crashing into other pieces of armor. Metal plates and weapons clattered to the floor.

Jack lay on the floor in the dark. He tried to get up. But his head was too heavy.

He heard deep voices.

Someone grabbed him by the arm. The next thing he knew, his helmet was yanked off. He was staring into the fiery light of a torch.

CHAPTER SIX

TA-DA!

In the torchlight, Jack saw three huge men standing over him.

One with very squinty eyes held the torch. One with a very red face held Jack. And one with a very long mustache held on to Annie.

Annie was kicking and yelling.

"Stop!" said the one with the very long mustache.

"Who art thou?" said the one with the very red face.

"Spies? Foreigners? Egyptians? Romans? Persians?" said the squinty-eyed one.

"No, you dummies!" said Annie.

"Oh, brother," Jack muttered.

"Arrest them!" said Red Face.

"The dungeon!" said Squinty Eyes.

The guards marched Jack and Annie out of the armory.

"Go!" said a guard, giving him a push.

Jack went.

Squinty, Annie, Mustache, Jack, and Red marched down the long, dark hallway. They marched down a narrow, winding staircase.

Jack heard Annie shouting at the guards. "Meanies! We didn't do anything!"

The guards laughed.

At the bottom of the stairs was a big iron door with a bar across it. Squinty lifted the bar. He shoved the door, and it creaked open.

Mustache and Red pushed Jack and Annie into a cold, clammy room.

The fiery torch lit the dungeon. There were chains hanging from the filthy walls. Water dripped from the ceiling, making puddles on the stone floor. It was the creepiest place Jack had ever seen.

"We'll keep them here till the feast is done. Then turn them over to the duke," said Squinty. "He knows how to take care of thieves."

"There will be a hanging tomorrow," said Mustache.

"If the rats don't get them first," said Red.

They all laughed.

Jack felt his backpack move. Annie was quietly opening it.

"Come on, let's chain the two of 'em," said Squinty.

The guards started toward Jack and Annie. Annie whipped her flashlight out of Jack's pack.

"Ta-da!" she yelled.

The guards froze. They stared at the shiny flashlight in Annie's hand.

Annie switched on the light. The guards gasped. They jumped back against the wall.

Squinty dropped the torch. It fell into a dirty puddle on the floor, sputtered, and went out.

"My magic wand!" Annie said, waving the flashlight. "Get down. Or I'll wipe you out!"

Jack's mouth dropped open.

Annie fiercely pointed her light at Squinty, then at Mustache, and then at Red. Each howled and covered his face.

"Down! All of you! Get down!" shouted Annie.

One by one, the guards knelt down on the wet floor.

Jack couldn't believe it.

"Come on," Annie whispered to Jack. "Let's go now."

Jack looked at the open doorway. He looked at the guards quaking on the ground.

"Hurry!" said Annie.

In one quick leap, Jack followed Annie out of the terrible dungeon.

CHAPTER SEVEN

A SECRET PASSAGE

Annie and Jack raced back up the winding stairs and down the long hallway.

They hadn't gone far when they heard shouting behind them.

Dogs barked in the distance.

"They're coming!" Annie cried.

"In here!" said Jack. He shoved open a door off the hallway and pulled Annie into a dark room.

Jack pushed the door shut. Then Annie

shined her flashlight around the room. There were rows of sacks and wooden barrels.

"I'd better look in the book," said Jack, pulling out the book and flipping through the pages.

"Shhh!" said Annie. "Someone's coming."

Jack and Annie jumped behind the door as it creaked open.

Jack held his breath. A light from a torch danced wildly over the sacks and barrels.

The light disappeared. The door slammed shut.

"Oh, man," whispered Jack. "We have to hurry. They might come back."

His hands were trembling as he turned the pages of the castle book.

"Here's a map of the castle," he said. "Look, this must be the room we're in. It's a storeroom." Jack studied the room in the book. "These are sacks of flour and barrels of wine."

"Who cares? We have to go!" said Annie. "Before they come back!"

"No. Look," said Jack. He pointed at the map. "There's a trapdoor."

He read aloud:

In this castle, a trapdoor led from the storeroom through a secret passage to a precipice over the moat.

"What's a precipice?" said Annie.

"I don't know. We'll find out," said Jack. "But first we have to find the trapdoor."

Jack looked at the picture carefully. Then he shined the flashlight around the room.

The floor of the room was made of stones. The trapdoor in the picture was five stones from the door to the hallway.

Jack shined the light on the floor and

counted the stones out loud. "One, two, three, four, five."

He stamped on the fifth stone. It was loose!

Jack put the flashlight on the floor. He worked his fingers under the thin slab of stone and tried to lift it.

"Help," Jack said. "It's heavy!"

Annie helped Jack lift the stone square out of its place. Underneath was a small wooden door.

Jack and Annie tugged on the rope handle of the door. The door fell open with a *thunk*.

Jack picked up the flashlight and shined it down the hole.

"There's a little ladder," he said. "Let's go!"

He clipped the flashlight onto his belt and felt his way down the small ladder. Annie followed.

When they reached the bottom of the

ladder, Jack shined the light around them.

There was a tunnel!

Jack crouched down and began moving through the damp, creepy tunnel. The flashlight dimly flickered across the stone walls.

He shook the light. Were the batteries going dead?

"I think our light's dying!" he said to Annie.

"Hurry!" she called from behind him.

Jack went faster. His back hurt from crouching.

The light got dimmer and dimmer. Jack was desperate to get out of the castle before the batteries died completely.

Soon he reached another small wooden door. It was the door at the end of the tunnel!

Jack unlatched the door and pushed it open.

He poked his head outside.

He couldn't see anything in the misty darkness.

The air felt cool and fresh. He took a deep breath.

"Where are we?" whispered Annie behind him. "What do you see?"

"Nothing. But I think we've come to the outside of the castle," said Jack. "I'll find out."

Jack put the flashlight in his pack. He put the pack on his back. He stuck his hand out the door. He couldn't feel the ground. "I'm going to have to go feet first," he said.

Jack turned around in the small tunnel. He lay down on his stomach. He stuck one leg out the door. Then the other.

Jack inched down, bit by bit, until he was hanging out the door, clinging to the ledge.

"This must be the precipice!" he called to Annie. "I can't touch the ground. Pull me up!"

Annie reached for Jack's hands. "I can't hold you!" she said.

Jack felt his fingers slipping. Then down he fell through the darkness.

SPLASH!

CHAPTER EIGHT

THE KNIGHT

Water filled Jack's nose and covered his head. His glasses slipped off. He grabbed them just in time. He coughed and flailed his arms.

"Jack!" Annie was calling from above.

"I'm in . . . the moat!" said Jack, gasping for air. He tried to tread water and put his glasses back on. With his backpack, his shoes, and his heavy clothes, he could barely stay afloat.

SPLASH!

"Hi! I'm here!" Annie sputtered.

Jack could hear Annie nearby, but he couldn't see her.

"Which way's land?" Annie asked.

"I don't know! Just swim!"

Jack dog-paddled through the cold black water.

He heard Annie swimming, too. At first it seemed as if she was swimming in front of him. But then he heard a splash behind him.

"Annie?" he called.

"What?" Her voice came from in front. *Not behind.*

Another splash. *Behind.*

Jack's heart almost stopped. *Crocodiles?* He couldn't see anything through his water-streaked glasses.

"Annie!" he whispered.

"What?"

"Swim faster!"

"But I'm here! I'm over here! Near the edge!" she whispered.

Jack swam through the dark toward her voice. He imagined a crocodile slithering after him.

Jack's hand touched a wet, live thing.

"Ahhhh!" he cried.

"It's me! Take my hand!" said Annie.

Jack grabbed her hand. She pulled him to the edge of the moat. They crawled over an embankment onto the wet grass.

"Oh, man," Jack said.

He was shivering all over. His teeth were chattering. He shook the water off his glasses and put them back on.

It was so misty he couldn't see the castle. He couldn't even see the moat, much less a crocodile.

"We . . . we made it," said Annie. Her teeth were chattering, too.

"I know," said Jack. "But where are we?" He peered at the foggy darkness.

Where was the drawbridge? The windmill? The hawk house? The grove of trees? The tree house?

Everything had been swallowed up by the thick, soupy darkness.

Jack reached into his wet backpack and pulled out the flashlight. He pushed the switch. Nothing happened. The batteries were dead.

They were trapped, but not in a dungeon. They were trapped in the still, cold darkness.

Neeee-hhhh!

A horse's whinny echoed through the night.

The clouds parted. A full moon was shining in the sky. A pool of light spread through the mist.

Jack and Annie saw a shadowy figure just a few feet away. It was the knight.

The knight sat on the black horse. His armor shone in the moonlight. A visor hid his face, but he seemed to be staring straight at Jack and Annie.

CHAPTER NINE

UNDER THE MOON

Jack froze.

"It's him," Annie whispered.

The knight held out his gloved hand.

"Come on, Jack," Annie said.

"Where are you going?" said Jack.

"He wants to help us," said Annie.

"How do you know?" said Jack.

"I can just tell," said Annie.

Annie stepped toward the horse. The knight dismounted.

The knight picked Annie up and put her on the back of his horse.

"Come on, Jack," Annie called.

Jack moved slowly toward the knight. The knight lifted him up, too, and put him on the horse, behind Annie.

The knight then got on behind them. He slapped the reins.

The black horse cantered beside the moonlit water of the moat.

Jack rocked back and forth in the saddle. The wind blew his hair. He felt very brave and very powerful.

He felt as if he could ride forever on this horse, with this mysterious knight, over the ocean, over the world, over the moon.

A hawk shrieked in the darkness.

"There's the tree house," said Annie. She pointed toward a grove of trees.

The knight guided the horse toward the trees.

"See. There it is," Annie said, pointing to the ladder.

The knight brought his horse to a stop. He dismounted and helped Annie and Jack down.

"Thank you, sir," Annie said. She bowed.

"Thank you," Jack said. He bowed, too.

The knight got back on his horse. He raised his gloved hand. Then he slapped the reins and rode off through the mist.

Annie started up the tall ladder, and Jack followed. They climbed into the dark tree house and looked out the window.

The knight was riding toward the outer wall of the castle. They saw him go through the outer gate.

Clouds started to cover the moon again. For a brief moment, Jack thought he saw the knight's armor gleaming on the top of a hill beyond the castle.

The clouds covered the moon completely. A black mist swallowed the land.

"He's gone," whispered Annie.

Jack shivered in his wet clothes as he kept staring at the blackness.

"I'm cold," said Annie. "Where's the Pennsylvania book?"

Jack heard Annie fumbling in the darkness. He kept looking out the window.

"I think this is it," said Annie. "I feel a silk bookmark."

Jack was only half-listening. He was hoping to see the knight's armor gleam again in the distance.

"Okay. I'm going to use this," said Annie. "Because I think it's the right one. Here goes. Okay. I'm pointing. I'm going to make a wish. I wish we could go to Frog Creek!"

Jack heard the wind begin to blow softly.

"I hope I pointed to the right picture in the right book," said Annie.

"What?" Jack looked back at her. "Right picture? Right book?"

The tree house began to rock. The wind got louder and louder.

"I hope it wasn't the dinosaur book!" said Annie.

"Stop!" Jack shouted at the tree house.

Too late.

The tree house started to spin.

It spun faster and faster!

Then everything was still.

Absolutely still.

CHAPTER TEN

ONE MYSTERY SOLVED

The air was warm.

It was dawn. Far away a dog barked.

"I think that's Henry barking!" Annie said.

Jack and Annie both looked out the tree house window.

"We're home!" said Annie. "Yay!"

"That was close," said Jack.

In the distance, streetlights glowed near their house. There was a light on in their upstairs window.

"Uh-oh," said Annie. "I think Mom and Dad are up. Hurry!"

"Wait." In a daze, Jack opened his pack. He pulled out the castle book. It was quite wet. But Jack placed it back with all the other books.

"Come on!" said Annie. She started climbing out of the tree house.

Jack followed her down the rope ladder.

They reached the ground and took off running between the gray-black trees.

They left the woods and ran down their quiet street.

They got to their yard and crept across the lawn.

They opened the front door carefully and slipped inside their house.

"They're not downstairs yet," whispered Annie.

"Shhh," said Jack.

He led the way up the stairs and down the hall. There was no sign of their mom or dad, but Jack could hear water running in the bathroom.

Their house was so different from the dark, cold castle. It was safe and cozy and friendly.

Annie stopped at her bedroom door. She gave Jack a smile, then disappeared inside her room.

Jack hurried into his room. He took off his damp clothes and pulled on his dry, soft pajamas.

He sat down on his bed and opened his backpack. He took out his wet notebook. He felt around for the pencil, but his hand touched something else.

Jack pulled the blue leather bookmark out of his pack. It must have fallen out of the castle book.

Jack held the bookmark close to his lamp and studied it. The leather was smooth and worn. It seemed ancient.

For the first time Jack noticed a letter on the bookmark. It was a fancy M.

Jack opened the drawer next to his bed. He took out the gold medallion.

He looked at the letter on it. It was the same M.

Now this *was an amazing new fact.*

Jack took a deep breath. At least that was one mystery solved.

The person who had dropped the gold medallion in the time of the dinosaurs was the same person who owned all the books in the tree house.

Who *was* this person?

Jack placed the bookmark next to the medallion. He closed the drawer.

Jack picked up his pencil. He turned to the least wet page in his notebook and started to write down this new fact.

the same

But before he could draw the M, his eyes closed.

Jack dreamed they were with the knight again. All three of them were riding the black horse through the cool, dark night. They rode beyond the outer wall of the castle and up over a moonlit hill.

Then they all rode into the mist.

Get the facts behind the fiction!
Magic Tree House® Fact Tracker
Dinosaurs

After their adventure in
the Cretaceous period, Jack and Annie
wanted to know more about dinosaurs.
Track the facts with them!

Turn the page for a sneak peek!

The biggest plant-eaters were the *sauropods* (SOAR-uh-pods). The sauropods left footprints as big as truck tires. They have names that mean things like "monster lizard" and "titanic lizard."

For many years, paleontologists thought the biggest dinosaur of all time was a sauropod called *Brachiosaurus* (BRACK-ee-uh-SOAR-us).

Brachiosaurus was as long as three school buses. But now, fossil hunters have found bones of three dinosaurs that were even bigger:

Big ➤

- *Supersaurus* (SOO-per-SOAR-us), which means "super lizard";

Really ➤ big

- *Ultrasaurus* (ULL-truh-SOAR-us), which means "extreme lizard";

Really, really ➤ big!

- *Seismosaurus* (SIZE-muh-SOAR-us), which means "earth-shaking lizard."

Stegosaurus
(STEG-uh-SOAR-us)

This name means "roofed lizard."

Stegosaurus was about the size of a mini-van. It had four long spikes on the end of its tail. It had big, flat plates growing out of its back.

Stegosaurus had a very small head. For many years, most books described *Stegosaurus* as having a brain the size of a golf ball. But paleontologists now think that *Stegosaurus*'s brain looked more like a hot dog!

Stegosaurus brain

Hot dog

Long tail spikes

Flat back plates

Huge body

Tiny head

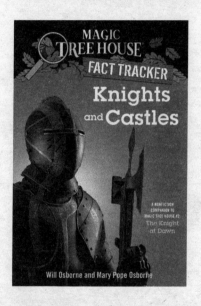

There's a mysterious tree house in the woods. It's filled with magic, books . . . and something prehistoric!

Journey to the past in this newly illustrated edition of the first adventure in the Magic Tree House® series, perfect for reading aloud!

Magic Tree House®

Magic Tree House® Merlin Missions

Magic Tree House® Super Edition

#1: WORLD AT WAR, 1944

Magic Tree House® Fact Trackers

More Magic Tree House®

A WORLD OF MAGICAL READING ADVENTURES AWAITS YOUR CHILD!

Dragons, Pirates, Dinosaurs . . . Hawaii, Houdini, and More!

MAGIC TREE HOUSE™

KIDS' ADVENTURE CLUB
IS NOW ONLINE

THERE'S SO MUCH TO DO:

Kids can track their reading progress, collect passport stamps, earn rewards, join reading challenges to unlock special prizes, and travel the world with Jack and Annie.

Visit MagicTreeHouse.com
to register your child for the Kids' Adventure Club!